Th
of British Fantasy
Literature

By A J Dalton

Luna Press PUBLISHING

www.lunapresspublishing.com

ISBN-13: 978-1-911143-16-1

Acknowledgements

I would like to thank Nadine West for all her support, Mum and Dad for always being there, all of my readers for their faith, Marcus Gipps of Gollancz for the global book deal, and every author of fantasy literature mentioned in this exegesis for their vision, craft and inspiring words.

Contents

1. Abstract   1

2. Introduction   3

3. How traditional 'high fantasy' and later sub-genres each represent and respond distinctly to sociohistorical context   7

4. How 'metaphysical fantasy' specifically differs from preceding and subsequent sub-genres   26

5. How Empire of the Saviours further exemplifies 'metaphysical fantasy'   37

6. Conclusion   47

7. References   52

1. Abstract

The first chapter of this exegesis considers the sociohistorical context of the development of each of the various sub-genres of British fantasy literature, moving from the 'high fantasy' of Tolkien's *The Lord of the Rings*, through the nature-based fantasy of the 1960s, to the 'swords and planets' sci-fi crossover sub-genre of the 1970s, the 'epic fantasy' of the 1980s and 90s, the 'urban fantasy', 'flintlock fantasy', 'steampunk' and 'comedic fantasy' of the new millennium, the 'dark fantasy' and 'metaphysical fantasy' (the latter established by my various novels) of the mid to late 2000s, to the 'grimdark fantasy' and 'dystopian YA' of the 2010s. This chapter shows how each sub-genre is informed by, and reacts to, its own sociohistorical moment, and that each sub-genre in large part derives its distinctiveness from that unique moment.

The second chapter considers how second-world 'metaphysical fantasy' and first-world 'dark fantasy' share the same (Millennial) sociohistorical moment and therefore particular literary features. The chapter then analyses how 'metaphysical fantasy' is distinctly informed by, reacts to and differs from the preceding sub-genre of second-world 'epic fantasy', while 'dark fantasy' is distinctly informed by, reacts to and differs from the preceding sub-genre of first-world 'urban fantasy', that analysis making clear the differences between 'metaphysical fantasy' and 'dark fantasy'. Finally, the chapter considers how subsequent 'grimdark fantasy' is informed by, reacts to and differs from 'metaphysical fantasy', and 'dystopian YA' is informed by, reacts to and differs from 'dark fantasy'.

The third chapter sets out how my novel *Empire of the Saviours* exemplifies 'metaphysical fantasy' and has served to establish the sub-genre as a distinct and valuable contribution to the wider genre of fantasy. Drawing upon *Empire of the Saviours*, the chapter identifies further literary features and themes (other than those detailed in the second chapter) that are unique to the 'metaphysical fantasy' sub-genre.

2. Introduction

I coined the term 'metaphysical fantasy' as it applies to literature in January 2008, when I established the www.metaphysicalfantasy.wordpress.com (www.ajdalton.eu) website to coincide with the release of my self-published novel *Necromancer's Gambit* in February 2008. The novel bore a gold badge on the cover declaring it 'The best of Metaphysical Fantasy'.

I coined the term for two main reasons: i) as a marketing ploy, via which I would 'own' a new sub-genre and ii) as a way of distinguishing the novel as offering something new and distinct to the wider genre. Before making the costly[1] decision to self-publish, I had submitted *Necromancer's Gambit* to every major publisher of fantasy, but had been universally rejected with statements including 'It's too dark' and 'It doesn't fit squarely within the genre'[2]. Ironically, the book's own originality and difference from the norm within

---

1. In this pre-Kindle era, self-publishing was far from a cheap option – I paid £2,000 to Authorhouse to see *Necromancer's Gambit* 'published', placed in Waterstones stores and represented on book-selling websites.
2. References are commercial-in-confidence.

the genre (from what was selling at the time) was considered its weakness by the leading publishers.

Necromancer's Gambit was rapidly taken up by a number[3] of Waterstones stores and the title began to sell in volume, despite it having a black cover, at a time when the white covers of Trudi Canavan's titles[4] had become the standard in the genre. Come November 2008, the *Twilight* movie arrived in cinemas and the new sub-genre term of 'dark fantasy' became popularised[5]. By the end of 2008, *Necromancer's Gambit* had become Waterstones's second biggest selling fantasy title (after *Twilight*) in the north-west region of England.

In 2011, based on both the considerable sales of *The Flesh & Bone Trilogy* (of which *Necromancer's*

---

3. Within six months of release, Necromancer's Gambit was in approximately forty stores, having initially been only placed in one store.
4. *The Magicians' Guild* (2004), *The Novice* (2005), *The High Lord* (2005).
5. To the extent that Waterstones soon introduced 'Dark Fantasy' book sections in stores, as evidenced by Anne Perry on the Hodderscape website: '**Ewa** has nerded thoroughly since the tender age of five, when some fool let her get her get her hands on a copy of *The Lion, The Witch & The Wardrobe*. Things progressed rapidly. Film footage exists of her sitting under the table at a birthday party, aged 11, where she hid in order to finish Stephen King's *IT*. She now runs the Sci Fi, Fantasy, Horror & **Dark Fantasy** sections in a small but perfectly formed Waterstones in central London (and still can't quite believe someone lets her) and tweets far too much about general geek matters at @EwaSR.'

Gambit was the first title) and the 'freshness'[6] offered by 'metaphysical fantasy', Gollancz, the UK's leading publisher of fantasy and sci-fi, gave me a three-book deal for *Chronicles of a Cosmic Warlord. Empire of the Saviours*, the first title in *Chronicles of a Cosmic Warlord*, was published in the UK in 2012. It was also sold to Blanvalet (Random House) in Germany in 2012, and was long-listed for the BFS National Fantasy Award (The Gemmell Award) in 2013. All this marked the arrival (and ultimate acceptance) of 'metaphysical fantasy' within the pantheon of established sub-genres of fantasy literature.

The definition, attitude, themes, motifs and linguistic styling of 'metaphysical fantasy' are broadly outlined on the Metaphysical Fantasy website, and the description is further developed in 'A note from the author' at the back of *Empire of the Saviours.* However, a better or more complete understanding of what 'metaphysical fantasy' uniquely represents can be arrived at via i) a consideration of how traditional 'high fantasy' and later sub-genres each represent and respond distinctly to sociohistorical context ii) a consideration of how 'metaphysical fantasy' specifically differs from preceding and subsequent sub-genres and iii) a consideration of Empire of the Saviours in terms of

6. An email from Marcus Gipps, commissioning editor at Gollancz, to A J Dalton, August 2011.

how it further exemplifies 'metaphysical fantasy'. This exegesis is intended as such a consideration and as a description of the distinctiveness of the 'metaphysical fantasy' novel *Empire of the Saviours*.

3. Chapter one: how traditional 'high fantasy' and later sub-genres each represent and respond distinctly to sociohistorical context

It is my argument that, in the same way that each sociohistorical period is distinct, the literature of each sociohistorical period can be seen to bear certain distinct features. In this chapter, I will give an overview of how the UK fantasy genre emerged and then developed over time, in order to exemplify, illustrate and demonstrate the distinctiveness of the fantasy of different periods[1]. Nearly every period that I will consider is typified by its own fantasy sub-genre, but it is of note that later periods actually exhibit an increasing number of their own sub-genres. This tendency within fantasy (of an increasing proliferation of sub-genres) reflects both the increasing degree to which each period reworks the original values, sub-genres and 'formulae' of fantasy, and the increasing pluralism/multiculturalism of the UK. The tendency is also a corollary of how

---

1. Also to produce a 'literature review' of the creative body of work that is British fantasy literature, thereby to contextualise the 'metaphysical fantasy' sub-genre.

the writing of fantasy works creatively to produce
literature that (while recognisable to readers of the
genre and its sub-genres) is still relevant, original and
distinct. 'Metaphysical fantasy' is just one example of
the creative work that is required and undertaken (as a
response to sociohistorical period) in order to produce
current, original and distinct genre-specific fiction.

Works throughout history, from *Gilgamesh*, to *The
Iliad*, *Beowulf*, Spenser's The Faerie Queene, various
tales of St George, and Walpole's *The Castle of
Otranto*[2], to name but a few, have contained fantastical
(monstrous and magical) elements. In large part,
however, such literary works[3] have represented socio-
religious allegory or used such elements to represent
divine will or moral test. In terms of English language
literature, it was not really until the nineteenth century
that such elements were used outside of a religious
framework of meaning. It was at this time that science,
and the character of the scientist, began to replace
God as the driving and organising function within
literary narrative. By way of example, we have Mary
Shelley's *Frankenstein: The Modern Prometheus*
(1818), Polidori's *The Vampyre* (1819), Verne's *Twenty*

---

2. The first novel to term itself 'gothic'.
3. As opposed to fairy tale narratives from a pre-Christian oral tradition,
narratives that were later re-codified within a Christian framework by the
likes of Charles Perrault and the brothers Grimm.

Thousand Leagues under the Sea (1870)[4], Stevenson's *The Strange Case of Dr Jekyll and Mr Hyde* (1886), H. G. Wells's *The Time Machine* (1895) and Bram Stoker's *Dracula* (1897). The latter is particularly interesting because the character of Dracula, albeit that he is depicted as a latter day Satan, created when breaking his relationship with God, and possessing of a terrifying capacity to take on new knowledge (as per the Tree of Knowledge) and different physical forms, is ultimately undone by the modern (Victorian era) technologies of communication, transportation and weaponry. There is a sense of humankind having developed the capacity and tools to exceed and overcome their own circumstance and limited place in the scheme of things. Indeed, the scheme of things is now more decided by humankind's own ego and desire. No longer does humankind look outward or 'upward' for salvation. Now humankind looks inward for a more creative inspiration and salvation, precisely at a time when Freud is publishing *Studies on Hysteria* (1895), the precursor to *The Interpretation of Dreams* (1899). Indeed, there is much in *Dracula* concerning the mastering of one's own mind if social and physical health, propriety and stability are to be maintained – the character of Mina, under the psychological sway of

---

4. Translated for the English-reading audience in 1873.

Dracula, becomes drawn and distant, jeopardising her proposed marriage and future prospects; and Dracula's mentally fraught servant Renton has to be shut in an asylum for the safety of himself and others.

All of the above literature recognised, predicted and described the wondrous and liberating future that science could allow us to achieve (heralding the genre of sci-fi). It also foresaw the horrors that it might bring upon us, or out of us, just as H. G. Wells's *War of the Worlds* (1898) anticipated World War I. Indeed, it was in the context of World War I that J. R. R. Tolkien began working on the world and mythology of the archetypal fantasy *The Lord of the Rings*, a work that rejected science and slavish armies as any sort of salvation, instead celebrating 'fellowship'[5] and more essential[6] human values such as self-sacrifice, loyalty, empathy and redemption. In refusing to include science, and instead exploring the motivations that would see all the tribes of the world march to war, *The Lord of the Rings* represented a remove from the real world (first-world[7]) so that a more spiritual consideration of it could take place, a consideration that saw human will and spirit

---

5. As in *The Fellowship of the Ring*, which sees a small and loyal group of friends triumph against all odds.

6. Within a Catholic moral framework, and in as far as Tolkien searches for our shared or commons roots in terms of the various tribes and languages of *The Lord of the Rings*.

7. 'First-world fantasy' is set in what is ostensibly the 'real' world.

manifested as a magical force. As pretty much the first literature to reject the reality of the scientific world (first-world) in preference for a magical one (second-world[8]), *The Lord of the Rings* represented the first mythology-based, second-world, 'modern'[9], 'adult'[10] fantasy novel[11].

The work of Tolkien is also commonly described as representing/defining the sub-genre of 'high fantasy'[12]. Its endeavour is far from trivial; it takes itself seriously. There is very little humour present within this sub-genre[13], for the quest undertaken by the protagonists is a moral one, a quest to save the world from itself, a quest of self-sacrifice and a quest for redemption (as Gollum sacrifices himself with the One Ring to

---

8. 'Second-world fantasy' makes no pretence about creating its own world, a world that obeys different laws to our own, a world where the laws of physics are largely replaced by magical laws and systems.

9. By which I mean post-Industrial Revolution.

10. As opposed to the Young Adult (YA) first-world becoming second-world fantasy of C. S. Lewis's *The Lion, The Witch and the Wardrobe* (1950).

11. In terms of release date Robert E. Howard's Conan short stories (1932 onwards) predated both *The Hobbit* and *The Lord of the Rings*, yet only appeared in Weird Tales magazine, lacked the wider conception required of a novel, tended to see magic as the unnatural artifice or 'science' of the antagonist and lacked the developed mythology of *The Lord of the Rings*.

12. Stableford, B. (2005). *The A to Z of Fantasy Literature*. Plymouth: Scarecrow Press, p. 198.

13. Particularly when compared to the work of fantasy authors like Terry Pratchett.

frustrate the Satanic Sauron and ultimately allow Frodo to win through, Gollum by his actions thereby repents his 'original', Cain-and-Abel sin concerning the ring). *The Lord of the Rings*, therefore, is set within a clear moral and religious framework, one that does not see science as necessary or meaningful to its narrative. The protagonist Frodo is the most consistently moral and self-sacrificing of the characters, and therefore triumphs despite his diminutive size and lack of physical strength. His Christ-like, self-sacrificing virtue is that which saves the world. He navigates the fraught quest of what is known in fantasy as the 'Chosen One'[14]. The moral and religious framework of *The Lord of the Rings* is not just clear from the allegorical plotting and characterisation, but also from the use of an omniscient narrator to set the scenes of chapters. More often than not a scene from nature is the setting, but a setting that works as either sympathetic background or foreshadowing of the moral challenges ahead. This approach to narrative perspective requires a single, epic world-view defined by a particular set of values, a set of values in Tolkien's case which are entirely Christian.

---

14. Komarck, M. (2015). *In Defence of the Chosen One*. Available at: http://fantasy-faction.com/2015/in-defence-of-the-chosen-one, (Accessed: 11 July 2016).

Even as Pippin gazed in wonder the walls passed from looming grey to white, blushing faintly in the dawn; and suddenly the sun climbed over the eastern shadow and sent forth a shaft that smote the face of the City. Then Pippin cried aloud, for the Tower of Ecthelion, standing high within the topmost walls shone out against the sky, glimmering like a spike of pearl and silver, tall and fair and shapely, and its pinnacle glittered as if it were wrought of crystals; and white banners broke and fluttered from the battlements in the morning breeze and high and far he heard a clear ringing as of silver trumpets. (The Return of the King, p. 12)

'High fantasy', then, is far from trivial in its consideration, for it offers comment on the moral condition of all humankind. Therefore, even though the story of *The Lord of the Rings* is set in a second world, it is a clear response to the happenings of the first world and its sociohistorical era. In important ways it is a response to, and commentary upon, the moral significance of World War I. A devout Roman Catholic and one member of a group of four childhood friends (reminiscent of the Fellowship of the Ring), Tolkien went to fight in France during World War I and saw his friends and battalion massacred at Orvillers[15]. In a later letter, Tolkien described how he began writing the language and mythology of *The Lord of the Rings* in canteens, crowded wooden huts, 'by candle light in bell-tents, even […] down in dugouts under shell fire'[16]. In 1916 he contracted trench fever, suffered delirium and was returned to Britain. By 1917 he had recovered and immediately began to write tales that later became *The Silmarillion* (1977). In another letter, Tolkien acknowledged: 'The Dead Marshes and the approaches to the Morannon owe something to Northern France after the Battle of the Somme'[17]. The Dead Marshes in *The Lord of the Rings* saw young, fallen soldiers sunk in pools and staring up, all unseeing, at the sky. They are at once as still and beautiful as they are horrific and challenging.

The Hobbit was published in 1937 and *The Lord of the Rings* finally in 1954. The themes of the work that had begun during World War I remained relevant and current through World War II and into the post-war era, an era typified by the Cold War, McCarthyism and the 1951 Burgess and Maclean scandal. *The Lord*

15. Carpenter, H. (1977). *J. R. R. Tolkien: A Biography*. New York: Ballantine Books.
16. Carpenter, H. and Tolkien, C. (eds.) (1981). *The Letters of J. R. R. Tolkien*. London: George Allen & Unwin. Letter 66, p. 90.
17. Op. cit. [16], Letter 226, p. 321.

of the Rings has clear themes of war, propaganda and ideological subversion (with the Wormtongue character), espionage (with the 'eye' of Sauron, and the spying treachery of Gollum), and the occupying invader (ending with the Shire overrun). Such themes allowed *The Lord of the Rings*, although distinct as the first modern high fantasy, to sit with contemporaneous works that shared themes of invasion and espionage. One example is Lewis's *The Lion, the Witch and the Wardrobe* (1950), the Young Adult (YA) fantasy that starts first-world with wartime children being evacuated to the countryside, contains the spy character of Mr Tumnus and even has Edmund playing the double-agent. Examples from sci-fi of the time include the invasions of Wyndham's *The Day of the Triffids* (1951), Frank Hampson's *Dan Dare* (1950 onwards) and 'the enemy within' novel that is Wyndham's *The Midwich Cuckoos* (1957).

Where, however, British sci-fi continued to describe an apocalyptic anxiety concerning technology 'in the wrong hands', in the hands of those with an alien ideology and philosophy, British fantasy continued to offer hope in describing the moral virtues of self-sacrifice and self-knowledge, exploring our shared origins and values, and proposing a redemptive love of those who are different or who have wronged us[18]. It was not surprising therefore that, come the 1960s, the 'hippy' era and the time of 'free love', it was fantasy that was in the ascendency, with its nature-based, pagan-origin narratives. Significant titles included Susan Cooper's *Over Sea, Under Stone* (1965), book one of *The Dark is Rising Sequence*, Alan Garner's *The Owl Service* (1967) and Ursula Le Guin's *A Wizard of Earthsea* (1968)[19].

The situation began to change come the 1970s, however, for science had enabled the Moon Landing in 1969 and then brought us the contraceptive pill. Now science offered us new physical and social freedoms, rather than destruction and a Big Brother style of monitoring and control. Science brought us hope, and the 1970s became known for 'Golden Age sci-fi', a genre fiction that took a patriarchal delight in mixing new worlds and sexually available females. The book covers of the time famously displayed fully naked women, female aliens with three naked breasts, and 'out-of-this-world' male sexual fantasies, Michael Moorcock's *The Hollow Lands*, Brian Aldiss's *The Moment of Eclipse* and Jack Vance's *Trullion*, to name

---

18. Both Gollum and Edmund are thus redeemed.
19. Published by Parnassus Books in the US and by Victor Gollancz Ltd in the UK in the same year.

but a few[20]. In enabling the 'free love' that began in the 1960s, science ensured that, more than ever, such love did not necessarily come with the consequence of children, the responsibility of parenthood, or the immediate need to marry, find a good job, buy a house and socially conform. It is of little surprise, therefore, that sci-fi was so dominant during this decade. Indeed, it was so dominant that fantasy literature was mostly successful in the first half of the decade as sci-fi-fantasy crossover (the 'swords and planets' sub-genre), as exemplified by John Norman's *Gorean Saga*, Michael Moorcock's *Eternal Champion Sequence* and the *Doctor Who* novels of the time.

With Margaret Thatcher becoming UK Prime Minister in 1979, Ronald Reagan becoming US President on behalf of the Republicans in 1981, and the HIV/AIDS epidemic first coming to prominence among gay men in the US in 1981[21], the patriarchal era of 'free love' came to an end. There was a return to earlier values[22], with the Prime Minister espousing individualism and responsibility – individuals working

---

20. TV and film of the time also gave us the likes of Star Trek and UFO, in which women wore mini-skirts and were highly sexualised.

21. AIDS.gov. (2011). *A Timeline of HIV/AIDS*. Available at: https://www.aids.gov/hiv-aids-basics/hiv-aids-101/aids-timeline/, (Accessed: 11 July 2016).

22. In an interview in *Headway Upper-Intermediate*, Margaret Thatcher describes those values as 'Victorian'.

hard and making sacrifice to build small businesses, acquire wealth and then contribute back to society. It was in this context that fantasy resurged in popularity, with 'epic fantasy' as the new dominant sub-genre[23]. This sub-genre tended to take a working-class hero ('The Magician's Apprentice') as the protagonist, as in David Eddings's *Pawn of Prophecy* (1982) or Raymond E. Feist's *Magician* (1982), and send them on a 'Chosen One' quest to save the world. Through hard work and moral virtue, they succeed and are invariably rewarded with a rise in social status and privilege, becoming a close friend and advisor to the royal family or a member of the magic elite. This plot line, of course, echoed Margaret Thatcher's personal and political story of having started out as a grocer's daughter, having fought to become a success in a man's world and having finally triumphed to become Prime Minister, thereby representing the positive and enlightened change in British society. At the same time, the plot fit with the Reaganomics version of the American Dream.

Where 'high fantasy' had had a religious framework,

---

23. There were complementary and variant sub-genres, including David Gemmell's 'heroic fantasy' (1984 onwards), building upon the earlier tradition of Robert E. Howard's Conan stories, with 'sword-and-sorcery' movies like *Conan the Barbarian* (1982) particularly popular in the cinema, and the 'role-playing-game fantasy' of *Dungeons & Dragons* and *Fighting Fantasy* (1982 onwards).

'epic fantasy' had a stronger social framework and indulged in more detailed world-building, with socio-economic systems in place, a clear divide between rural and urban areas and functions, a sense of social class and place, and so on. Where 'high fantasy' had one true God or an enemy embodying absolute evil, 'epic fantasy' presented a more multicultural pantheon of gods and a range of roguish and morally-compromised characters. Where 'high fantasy' was largely humourless, 'epic fantasy' offered the gentle humour and banter of social negotiation, without that humour ever becoming fully subversive (unless it is used as a weapon against the enemy, as in Stephen Donaldson's *Lord Foul's Bane*[24], 1977). Where 'high fantasy' ended with the main characters restored to the safety and peace of their home, 'epic fantasy' promised, encouraged and allowed social advancement based on particular behaviours. Where there are precious few female characters in 'high fantasy', there are a good deal more in 'epic fantasy', albeit rarely in the main role. What the two sub-genres of fantasy had in common, however, was a lack of anything sexually explicit, along with the presumption that those at the top of society were only there based upon some moral superiority (be that religious virtue or a sense of social

---

24. This book had 'An Epic Fantasy' on the cover, effectively as a sub-title.

responsibility).

Entering the 1990s, the Conservative Margaret Thatcher was replaced with the Conservative John Major as Prime Minister and, in the US, the Republican Ronald Reagan was replaced by the Republican George Bush as President. 'Epic fantasy', with its twin promises of individual reward and social advancement, remained dominant. Male authors like Donaldson, Eddings and Feist continued to be successful, and new ones arrived, such as Terry Goodkind (*Wizard's First Rule*, 1994) and L. E. Modesitt Jr (*The Saga of Recluce*, beginning 1991), but this decade also saw a significant increase in the number of female authors of this sub-genre being published. By way of example, in the UK there were J. V. Jones (*The Baker's Boy*, 1995), Maggie Furey (*The Artefacts of Power*, beginning 1994) and Juliet E. McKenna (*The Thief's Gamble*, 1999), to name the most prominent, and in the US there were the likes of Robin Hobb (*Assassin's Apprentice*, 1995), Mercedes Lackey (numerous contemporaneous series) and Marion Zimmer Bradley (*Black Trillium*, 1990). Indeed, such a proliferation represented how the popularity and dominance of 'epic fantasy' only increased during the 1990s, but it was probably the sub-genre's unusual longevity and degree of dominance that contributed to its eventual decline, for fantasy had become extremely 'formulaic'[25], if not entrenched, to the extent that it did not or could not adjust so easily to changes in society in order to remain relevant to readers. There was a sense that society and the genre were in denial or retrograde, and that there was a moment of truly horrific self-realisation on the horizon. The millennium was coming. We were faced with Y2K, all the machines stopping, and a new dark age for humanity. Science was about to bring us to our knees once more, so it was as if we were insisting upon the social and moral values of 'epic fantasy' as the only thing that might save us. We needed to remember who we were, to look back in order to identify what had made and defined our better selves. The fear was that, in our desperation, we were deluding ourselves.

The desire to 'look back' towards some lost golden age, in an attempt to remember our 'better selves', was very much reflected in the rising popularity of 'steampunk' sci-fi literature. The term 'steam-punks' was coined by K. Jeter in a letter to Locus magazine in 1987[26], but the term was not used in a book title until Paul Di Filippo's 1995 *Steampunk Trilogy*. Jeter

---

25. The term 'formulaic' is often used by readers of the genre I speak to (at my book signing events), publishing professionals and fantasy authors to describe the 'epic fantasy' of the 1990s, as seen on such websites as www.vision.ae and The Caffeinated Symposium.

26. Jeter, K. (1987). *Science Fiction Citations*. Available at: http://www.jessesword.com/sf/view/327, (Accessed: 11 July 2016).

was the author of the novel *Morlock Night* (1979), the title a direct reference to H. G. Wells's *Time Machine*, an indication that the values and optimism of the past tradition were being retrospectively embraced and reworked for a modern audience. This scifi sub-genre tended to use Victorian technology in a futuristic way, thereby introducing themes of 'alternative/alternate history', and was very much a counterpart to the 'flintlock fantasy'[27] of Stephen Hunt's 1994 *For the Crown and the Dragon*, in which the Napoleonic wars of Europe were instead fought with sorcery and steampunk technology.

The perhaps retrograde and rose-tinted natures of 'steampunk' and 'flintlock fantasy' were counter-balanced by the work of Sir Terry Pratchett and the 'urban fantasy' of the time. Pratchett spoofed the traditional motifs of fantasy (and sci-fi) to such an extent that he brought a new self-awareness to the wider genre, to 'have fun with some of the clichés'[28] in his own words. His *Discworld* series (the name playing off Larry Niven's successful *Ringworld* novel of 1970) parodied and played with real-world concerns like religion, film-

27. The term 'flintlock fantasy' coined by the reviewer Andrew Darlington in reference to Hunt's novel, as described in an interview with Hunt on The Book Plank website.
28. Young, J. (2005). Terry Pratchett on the Origins of Discworld, His Order of the British Empire and Everything in between, *Science Fiction Weekly*, 449.

making, rock and roll music, newspaper publishing and even the Gulf War, with the sort of healthy cynicism that the readership of the new millennium increasingly needed in order to feel grounded. The Discworld novel *Snuff* was the third-fastest selling hardback for adults since UK records had begun, selling 55,000 copies in its first three days of release. The sub-genre of 'urban fantasy' was popular at around the same time because it also 'grounded' fantasy and its readers, in that it was deliberately first-world, set in a familiar urban landscape, and offered a certain grittiness along with its fantastical or supernatural elements. More often than not, the plots revolve around some sort of serious crime (murder, kidnapping, assassination, etc.) or insidious threat (a shadowy mafia or creeping sort of corruption) that threatens not just the protagonist but also the wider society. A classic example of the genre is Neil Gaiman's *Neverwhere*, which was first aired as a BBC radio show in 1996 and released as a novel later the same year. The story is set in modern London and concerns Richard Mayhew, who suffers with both a dull job in business and an over-demanding fiancée. When he stops on the street one day to help a young, bleeding girl, his life changes forever as he is drawn into the parallel world of Neverwhere beneath the city, where he must confront monsters, saints, murderers and angels, to complete his quest to save the girl and himself[29]. Another seminal work of the sub-genre, but this one in TV and film, is *Buffy the Vampire Slayer*, which ran 1997-2004, in which the problems of modern, romantic relationships were key to grounding the characters and maintaining the sense of urban realism.

The proliferation and competition of 'steampunk', 'flintlock fantasy', 'comedic fantasy' and 'urban fantasy', with the arrival of the new millennium, marked the end of the numerous decades in which a single sub-genre dominated, represented or defined the genre, its social moment and its wider society. The fractures, class divides and competing groups and voices within society were becoming more obvious. Social certainties were replaced by social anxieties, and competing values now informed social and individual identity. The early 2000s surely foreshadowed and predicted the approaching crisis of 2008/09 onwards, the time of the credit crunch and the time during which UK politicians were found guilty en masse of the Expenses Scandal, the tabloid press were culpable in the Phone Hacking Scandal, and the police were found guilty of the Selling Information Scandal. No longer were we ruled and safeguarded by those of superior moral standing, of a noble conscience and

29. Gaiman, N. (no date). *Neverwhere*. Available at: http://www.neilgaiman.com/works/Books/Neverwhere/.

with a sense of social responsibility. No longer could the frameworks of 'high fantasy' and 'epic fantasy' be offered as valid. Now we were entering the age of 'metaphysical fantasy', 'dark fantasy', 'dystopian YA' and 'grimdark fantasy'.

4. Chapter two: how 'metaphysical fantasy' specifically differs from preceding and subsequent sub-genres

With the approaching credit crunch and the onset of the various corruption scandals previously mentioned, the first-world 'urban fantasy' of the early 2000s evolved into first-world 'dark fantasy'. Both sub-genres concern themselves with modern romantic relationships but, where 'urban fantasy' tends to observe patriarchal heterosexual norms (the good guy 'wins' the girl), 'dark fantasy' is more morally ambivalent, there are no out-and-out good guys and sexual congress is considered 'dangerous' and often to be resisted, i.e. everything is 'darker'. So, for example, where Joss Whedon's *Buffy the Vampire Slayer* (1997-2004) sees Buffy falling for (and making traditional, unthreatening love with) male vampires who invariably possess or seek a human soul, by contrast the lead female role of Bella in the *Twilight* series (2005-08), played in the movie by the gay Kristen Stewart, actively seeks a sexual relationship with Edward that is likely to destroy her. She is repeatedly reminded of the dangers of sexual consummation, and is almost killed by a subsequent pregnancy and childbirth ordeal, an ordeal that is described in truly horrific terms. Then, in *True Blood* (late 2008 onwards), we are presented with a far wider range of dark alternative relationships and lifestyles, from the abstinent, to S&M, to the pansexual, to the sinful, to the grotesque, to the fatal, to the drug-fuelled, to master-slave, to the orgiastic. Thus, the development from 'urban fantasy' to 'dark fantasy' represented mainstream society's anxiety concerning – and its getting to grips with – the true diversity of orientations, preferences and identities. With the elites and the establishment revealed as corrupt and morally redundant, the traditional heroes and values of society were abandoned and there was a turning to, representation of and 'acceptance' of other and more diverse voices in society (voices that had traditionally been marginalised, represented as socially undesirable or as belonging to 'the dark side').

In the same way that first world 'dark fantasy' represented the transition of first-world 'urban fantasy' to a more modern sociohistorical context, so second-world 'metaphysical fantasy' represented the transition of second-world 'epic fantasy' to a more modern consideration. Just as 'dark fantasy' brought darker themes, understanding and outlooks to 'urban fantasy', so 'metaphysical fantasy' did the same for 'epic fantasy'. Both 'metaphysical fantasy' and 'epic fantasy' concern themselves with the 'Chosen One' quest to save the world from evil forces but, where 'epic fantasy' tends to see the pre-existing social and moral order triumphantly restored (with the protagonist rewarded via social advancement), 'metaphysical fantasy' is more morally ambivalent in terms of the narrative outcome, there are no out-and-out winners (indeed, mere survival often comes at a hefty price) and social advancement is never quite the prize it is promised to be, i.e. everything is darker. So, for example, where the 'epic fantasy' novels of Raymond E. Feist's *Magician* (1982), David Eddings's *Pawn of Prophecy* (1984) and J. V. Jones's *The Baker's Boy* (1995) all see a good-hearted boy (the 'Chosen One') from the kitchens become friends with royalty while undertaking a quest that saves the world, reaffirms key social values and ennobles society, the 'metaphysical fantasy' novels of my own *Necromancer's Gambit* (2008) and *Empire of the Saviours* (2012) see a socially marginalised individual as 'Chosen One' go on a quest that defeats the enemy but also shatters society in the process[1]. Where 'epic fantasy' ends

1. Titles including Alan Campbell's *Scar Night* (2006) and R. Scott Bakker's *The Darkness That Comes Before* (2004) also fit this general plot shape, so the label 'metaphysical fantasy' might retrospectively be applied to them.

with glorious triumph and celebration, the 'triumph' at the end of 'metaphysical fantasy' is pyrrhic at best, all but genocidal or apocalyptic at worst. Where 'epic fantasy' self-congratulates and throws itself a party or feast, 'metaphysical fantasy' sees the protagonist left to bury the dead, grieve over loved ones and try to pick up the pieces of a broken world. Where 'epic fantasy' is about what can be won, 'metaphysical fantasy' is about what has been lost. Implicitly, then, where 'epic fantasy' endorses the society and values that determine success, 'metaphysical fantasy' explores, questions and even challenges them. Thus, the development from 'epic fantasy' to 'metaphysical fantasy', coinciding with the elites and establishment revealed as morally corrupt and redundant, represented society's increasing anxiety and discomfort concerning its traditional values, shamed heroes and so-called role models, as well as its treatment of socially marginalised groups; the development saw epic and ennobled heroes and social values abandoned in favour of those who had previously suffered heroically as marginalised individuals or groups.

So although 'dark fantasy' is first-world and deals with modern romantic relationships while 'metaphysical fantasy' is second-world and deals with social relationships and position, what these two sub-genres share (along with their sociohistorical moment) are a moral ambivalence and sense of anxiety. Where preceding sub-genres present unhesitating heroes acting with moral certainty, 'dark fantasy' and 'metaphysical fantasy' give us protagonists who are conflicted, compromised and self-doubting, protagonists who find it difficult always to know good from bad and to know who to trust, protagonists who are closer to 'anti-hero' than 'hero'. Where preceding sub-genres tend to be morally 'black and white', 'dark fantasy' and 'metaphysical fantasy' see everything in 'shades of grey' or as a matter of taking on a more plural, less simplistic perspective. By way of example, the protagonist Bella in the 'dark fantasy' *Twilight* finds herself in a town full of strangers and competing factions, all of which want to use her as much as help her; she is warned against each of them and, even when she specifically wishes to commit herself, is actively denied (for Edward will neither bite nor make love to her); she must doubt what she thought existed between herself and Edward, doubt her own judgement, doubt her understanding of love, life and meaning, and doubt herself as being anything other than sinfully attracted to a soulless and godless vampire. Similarly, the protagonist Jillan in the 'metaphysical fantasy' *Empire of the Saviours*, having killed a bullying classmate in self-defence but by using forbidden magicks, is forced to abandon his parents and flee his hometown, only then to encounter a range of strangers and factions that are more interested in using him for his corrupting power than in helping him; time and again he is forced to question the values and trust upon which his relationship with individuals and society are based, question his own judgement, examine his own deadly betrayal of fellowship, community and faith, and question himself as being anything other than sinfully obsessed with his own tainted and murderous self.

The protagonists of both first-world 'dark fantasy' and second-world 'metaphysical fantasy' therefore struggle for a sense of identity and existential meaning. Given that this 'crisis' of identity in the mid-to-late-2000s sits in stark contrast to the sense of moral and social certainty, superiority and security found pre-9/11 (2001), the move from 'epic fantasy' and 'urban fantasy' to 'dark fantasy' and 'metaphysical fantasy' can be understood as a corollary to the emergence and development of the 'Millennial'[2] self: an individual reaching young adulthood around the year 2000, sometimes known as 'Generation Y'. Where the generation preceding[3] the Millennial self could simply

---

2. The term was first coined by William Strauss and Neil Howe in 1987, and more fully described in their 1991 book *Generations: The History of America's Future*, which was followed in 2000 by *Millennials Rising: The Next Generation.*
3. 'Generation X'.

share in and espouse the traditional values of their parents and society (the 'epic fantasy' sub-genre was unusually dominant for the two decades before 2000), the Millennial self experienced a break or disconnect from (what had been) social reality. This disconnect is more often than not represented in 'dark fantasy' and 'metaphysical fantasy' as protagonists being exiled, abandoned, cast adrift or suffering the surreal experience of being the dead/undead in the world of the living. *Twilight* begins with Bella being taken to the airport in sunny Phoenix and boarding a plane to '*a small town named Forks* [which] *exists under a near-constant cover of clouds*' in order to live with her estranged father (*Twilight*, p. 2). *Empire of the Saviours* sees Jillan exiled from Godsend and separated from his parents in the first chapter. And *Necromancer's Gambit* opens with Saltar being raised from the dead against his will, both with little memory of who he previously was when alive and with an inability to trust the controlling necromancer who has fundamentally sinned in raising him. What these three examples also have in common, of course, is a disconnect with authority figures and wise counsellors, those who pass on the traditional values of society, promote conformity and ensure the individual's experience of the world is manageable and ultimately benign. Indeed, where Bella's parents are largely absent in *Twilight*, the kings and rulers in

Empire of the Saviours and *Necromancer's Gambit* are conspicuously corrupt, insidious and malign.

The plot progression of 'dark fantasy' and 'metaphysical fantasy' therefore involves the protagonist's fraught quest to discover a sense of identity and self, to find a place in the world, and to find safety and contentment. Invariably, however, these two sub-genres ultimately describe terrible sacrifice, loss, anti-climax and resignation. The self-realisation, place, safety and contentment that are achieved are illusory or temporary at best. There is no true 'happy ending', as the existential quest of life continues on through the next generation(s), some progress made but the results of past mistakes born into the future, the problems of society and the past inherited by those that follow on after us. In *The Twilight Saga*, the final battle which destroys both the protagonist Cullens and antagonist Volturi is anti-climactically revealed to be a mere foretelling, one which actually dissuades the Volturi from starting the battle at all (or postpones it to a more distant future), leaving Edward and Bella with their rapidly maturing hybrid daughter to their lives in the 'perfect peace' of their small cottage, lives that are surreal, sublimated and heavenly precisely because they cannot actually exist in the real world: '*And then we continued blissfully into this small but perfect piece of our forever*' (*Breaking Dawn*, p. 768). In my *Flesh*

& Bone Trilogy, the final scene has Mordius and Saltar discussing the essentially different and disruptive nature and inheritance of Saltar's son Orastes, how the people must eventually lose their faith in the gods, that the balance will fail, and that 'the damage is already done and that one day this realm must end' (*Necromancer's Fall*, p. 362). Finally, my *Chronicles of a Cosmic Warlord* end with a pregnant Hella asking Jillan if their child will be safe and her realising that '*If they're anything like their father, they'll still find ways to get into trouble*' (*Tithe of the Saviours*, p.365) ... and then the Epilogue presents us with the antagonist Declension successful once more in another realm ('*He would see the Declension claim the cosmos for itself*', p.368), with the Peculiar looking on: '*Still, wouldn't things be boring if they became too easy?*' (p.369).

'Dark fantasy' and 'metaphysical fantasy', then, do not ultimately provide 'solutions' to all the societal problems with which they contend. Although there is confrontation and accountability described, the problems are ultimately shared by all and continue into the future. In the UK, that future (the early 2010s) saw all of society apparently sharing in the pain of the credit crunch and austerity, but it soon became apparent that the pain was not being shared equally, that the rich were only becoming comparatively richer, that failed executives (arguably those responsible for the crash) were still receiving massive bonuses, and that it was the less privileged classes who were truly paying for the mistakes and greed of the privileged. (Neither should we forget the previously mentioned MPs' expenses scandal, the phone hacking scandal and the police selling of information scandal that were also ongoing.) The resentment, anger and disillusionment resulting from these revelations inevitably saw the 'dark fantasy' and 'metaphysical fantasy' of the late 2000s replaced with the 'dystopian YA' and 'grimdark fantasy' of the early 2010s.

Both near-future, first-world 'dystopian YA' and second-world 'grimdark fantasy' describe an immoral or lawless society in which those at the top are the most corrupt, immoral or bullying. There are themes of abuse, betrayal and abandonment present throughout both sub-genres. For example, in the 'dystopian YA' novels of *The Hunger Games Trilogy* (Collins, 2008-10), the *Escape from Furnace* series (Smith, 2009-11) and the *Maze Runner* series (Dashner, 2009-16), we are presented with death-match game shows featuring youth, the unjust imprisonment of youth, the institutionalised murder of youth, surgical experimentation on youth, and the use of youth as military fodder. Similarly, in the 'grimdark fantasy' novels of *A Song of Ice and Fire* (Martin, 1996-2016), *The Demon Cycle* series (Brett, 2008-16), *The Broken*

Empire Trilogy (Lawrence, 2011-13) and *The First Law* series (Abercrombie, 2006-16), we are routinely presented with torture, rape, brutalisation, the flaying of skin and mass slaughter. The sub-genres describe such horror unflinchingly, with a numb matter-of-factness or with a shocking sense of detachment; far from being voyeuristic, the literature is satirically post-traumatic, defiantly desensitised and utterly disillusioned. Indeed, the horror is so extreme but mundane that a profound sense of nihilism, mental exhaustion and an apocalyptic desire for self-destruction plagues all.

Yet hope is not entirely absent (particularly in 'dystopian YA'), for the existential quest of the defiant protagonist still drives the narrative of both sub-genres. 'Dystopian YA' tends to culminate in the youthful protagonist successfully escaping or destroying the institutions of the corrupt society, and even 'grimdark fantasy' offers us an anti-hero to introduce a new social order (albeit that the anti-hero often fails in their long-term aim). We might finally wonder how best to summarise the 'solution' offered by these two sub-genres. Some might describe it as 'civil war', some as anarchy and terrorism. Some might welcome such a solution, some might see it as inevitable and others still would advocate fighting to resist it. Perhaps that is another story, one for those with 2020 vision.

5. Chapter three: how Empire of the Saviours further exemplifies 'metaphysical fantasy'

As outlined in the previous chapter, 'metaphysical fantasy' concerns itself with the story of the self-doubting, Millennial protagonist experiencing 'a break or disconnect from (what had been) social reality'. Thereby, 'metaphysical fantasy' implicitly represents a break or disconnect from the Chosen One protagonist, definition of heroism[1], social and moral values, dominating ideology, authenticity and reality of 'epic fantasy'. For this reason, 'metaphysical fantasy' novels more often than not start with a description of the sort of well-ordered and thriving kingdom that would be found in an 'epic fantasy' novel, but then furnish the reader (via the protagonist) with a sense that there is something wrong, skewed, tainted or hidden. All is not as it seems, and the thing that is hidden is horrific, corrupt and malign. By way of example, in *Necromancer's Gambit*, King Voltar of Dur Memnos has outlawed the unholy magic of necromancy, apparently works to

---

1. The tagline to *Empire of the Saviours* is 'Heroes are not always what they seem'.

secure the sway of the loving Goddess of Creation and appears to protect the living from both the dead (led by their dark god Lacrimos) and the enemy kingdom of Accritania (led by their bloody priest Innius), but ultimately the King is unmasked as a necromancer involved in an ongoing genocide of the living, in his bid to achieve absolute sway over both life and death. In *Empire of the Saviours*, Jillan lives in the apparently safe community of Godsend, a town guarded by the Heroes of an empire of living Saints and Saviours, an empire and religious order which ostensibly holds back the Chaos; yet it emerges that the People are being kept prisoner so that they might be bled of all magic by the Saints and, in the long-term, all life by the parasitic Saviours.

In the 'metaphysical fantasy' plot, it then becomes apparent that the dominating ideology of the 'epic fantasy' kingdom is actively working to keep its malignancy and inadequacy hidden. In order to do this, the 'epic fantasy' kingdom asserts an insidious narrative or reality to blind, control and define all those within its society. In *Necromancer's Gambit*, that narrative is the lie of King Voltar, the laws he institutes (enforced by murderous Wardens and Guardians), the commands he issues to the army, and the word and will of his unholy magic. When that narrative is resisted by anyone (no matter whether they are the cowardly

Mordius, the needy Young Strap, the animated corpse Saltar, the emotionally damaged Kate or the friendless Scourge), it threatens all of society and the gods of creation themselves, resulting in an apocalyptic battle that sees reality itself unravel: ' *"Better this free choice than an eternity of slavery and self-abortion beneath the will of another," Saltar decided as he watched first his comrades and then Kate fade away*' (p. 367). Once the narrative and reality of 'epic fantasy' have unravelled and dissipated, a new narrative is constructed in the next chapter by the word and will of Saltar, one whose origin and nature have always belonged to a different (competing) realm and reality. In *Empire of the Saviours*, the dominating ideology and narrative are embodied by The Book of Saviours, the holy book of the rulers, which is the only text studied in school, a book that (re)writes the history of the People, and a book that absolutely cannot be questioned. When that narrative is questioned by anyone (be it a schoolboy in the farthest flung village of the Empire, a small number of pagans living in a remote mountain range, an old and friendless soldier, a woman suffering rock-blight while working as a slave in a mine, or an exiled, alcohol-dependent woodsman), it threatens all of society and must be suppressed at all costs, even if via a genocide of the People. Indeed, it is only once the apocalypse comes, in *Tithe of the Saviours*, that the dominating narrative is no longer required as there are no people left to control: '*It is of no consequence, for there is no consequence left to this realm. All has been said and all has been done. The Book of Saviours for this realm is now written and ended. There are no more words to follow. The pages of this realm's future are blank*' (p. 259, the three pages following being literally blank). Once that narrative has run its absolutist course and only the whispering dead remain, the new life, reality and narrative that manifest are born of an 'element' originating from beyond the empire and realm of the Saviours; Jillan (still in possession of creative magic) suicidally embraces sun-metal (actually the sentient element 'xi') and is 'resurrected' as the servant of xi, becoming a 'Cosmic Warlord' with the power to resist and defeat the previously dominating and defining power of the Saviours. '*As it ends, so it begins, over and over. It cannot be otherwise. Were it otherwise, absolutes would reign, and xi cannot allow that, for it would annihilate the cosmos, all realities and xi itself. Xi is the unstable element. Xi prevents the reign of absolutes. Xi cannot allow omniscience or omnipotence. Your death cannot yet be permitted*' (p. 301).

Within 'metaphysical fantasy', then, a corollary (or even consequence) of the 'epic fantasy' ideology and narrative framework unravelling is the undermining, fragmentation and unravelling of its physical reality. 'Metaphysical fantasy' literally goes *beyond* or *past*[2] the surface physicality of the 'epic fantasy' world in order to explore, question and challenge the fundamental, underpinning or larger ideas, values and psycho-construction of that world. Accordingly, the hidden truth of what is wrong with the 'epic fantasy' reality is glimpsed via altered states (as in *Necromancer's Gambit*, when Saltar finds himself in a hell-like realm every time he fights the monsters of King Voltar's magic and world) or via dream sequences (as in *Empire of the Saviours*, when Jillan sees Saint Azual sitting on a throne of skulls or is able to view and hear the Saviours' malign plotting). At the same time, alternative and competing realities are also presented: *The Flesh & Bone Trilogy* not only presents us with the demon realm but also all the realms accessed through The Prison of All Eternity; and *Chronicles of a Cosmic Warlord* presents us with the netherworld of the dead, the home realm of the Declension and at least eight other cosmic realms. As each of these realms has a distinct and differing nature, social order and philosophy of being, implicitly the physical is only a refraction, symptom or consequence of a spiritual or psychological state.

---

2. 'Meta-' as a prefix of the Greek language, translating as 'beyond, after or past'.

Essentially, the values and definition of the 'real' and meaningful as far as they are described by 'epic fantasy' are rejected by 'metaphysical fantasy'. The 'real' or physical world of 'epic fantasy' may be where 'metaphysical fantasy' starts, but it most certainly is not where 'metaphysical fantasy' ends. As 'metaphysical fantasy' is more concerned with the spiritual or psychological journey of its protagonists, it has no need of the geographical maps that are common to both 'high fantasy' and 'epic fantasy'. The maps which describe the latter two sub-genres create a measured physical reality for the 'natural' social order of their kingdoms, a reality and nature which 'metaphysical fantasy' subverts. Where the dark forests of 'high fantasy' and 'epic fantasy' harbour the monsters of the evil threatening the social order of 'good' but also friends who might aid the quest (e.g. elves), the dark forests of 'metaphysical fantasy' are psychologically disorientating, morally ambivalent and self-revelatory[3]. By brief way of example, in *Necromancer's Gambit*, when Mordius and Saltar have made their precipitous decision to set out, they all but immediately find that the main challenge they face is themselves: '*Just as his thoughts swam, Mordius felt he was having to swim his way through the Weeping Woods*' (p. 64). Similarly,

3. Similar to the role of forests in traditional fairy tales.

in *Empire of the Saviours*, having to leave Godsend because of accidentally killing a schoolmate, Jillan must immediately contend with himself in order to make progress: '*[H]e peered tiredly at the higgledy-piggledy graves and wondered where they would put Karl's body. If he'd had a flower, he'd have placed it in some open area. He half wanted to lie down with the dead himself, but this was not a cemetery for pagan bodies, so he dragged himself into the woods. After all, the bad things in this world were not deserving of a quick death, he'd been told*' (p. 28).

Indeed, unlike in 'epic fantasy', the main challenge for the protagonist in 'metaphysical fantasy' is the nature of the self, including both the physical and psychological aspects of the self. Thus, in *Necromancer's Gambit*, as an 'animee' (a type of zombie) Saltar physically embodies a magic that is outlawed and threatens the 'balance' between life and death as well as the divine and mortal, but he must also contend with the range of human emotions and desires as they are embodied by each of the gods (Shakri is love, Incarnus is hate, Aa is vain ambition, and so on). In *Empire of the Saviours*, Jillan's growing magic has not been 'Drawn' by his Saint, so Jillan physically embodies the magic that is forbidden to the People, and psychologically represents the 'taint' of the Chaos threatening the wider social order. Even more, then, the very existence of the protagonist is 'wrong' according to the world within which they find themselves, and as a consequence they are hunted and persecuted. Just the act of survival is a form of resistance and self-assertion which ultimately undoes the pre-existing reality and the pathologically self-obsessed and self-promoting rulers. The self-definition and self-empowerment of others seriously threatens the status quo, and therefore the population must be watched and controlled, and independent or wilful individuals must be exiled or executed. So, in *Necromancer's Gambit*, the people are controlled and continuously diminished in the way that all society is geared towards sacrificing generation after generation to the cause of a war-without-end, and in *Empire of the Saviours* the People are ideologically proscribed by the Minister in each community, mentally monitored by their Saints ('The Saint always knows!' is the refrain) and physically 'guarded' (safeguarded but also imprisoned) by their Heroes, the walls around their towns, curfews and the supposed threat beyond the walls.

Hence, far from helping to inform and define the individual, the pre-existing society (of 'epic fantasy') within 'metaphysical fantasy' works to suppress, erase or destroy individuality and free-thinking. Although the society presented is well-ordered, prosperous and peaceful, it is ultimately disempowering, predatory, parasitic (King Voltar literally wants to consume the beating Heart of all life, while the Eldest of the Saviours is revealed to be a grotesque mind-leech) and self-consuming. There is no place allowed for individual creativity or expression within the prescriptive social codes and hierarchy that represent 'epic fantasy'. What we are also describing here, then, is how the sub-genre of 'epic fantasy' (dominant and dominating for such an extraordinary length of time compared to other sub-genres) became essentially self-promulgating and 'formulaic'[4], allowed mainstream fantasy publishing to be dominated by particular authors, to the extent very few new authors like myself could break through[5], and ironically created the conditions for its own eventual demise. With the passing of its prolonged sociohistorical period, 'epic fantasy' became a largely redundant model for fantasy literature, the arrival of 'metaphysical fantasy' therefore marking the literal and literary death of 'epic fantasy'. In the end, the story and birth of 'metaphysical fantasy' is the story of

---

4. As mentioned previously, the term 'formulaic' is often used by readers of the genre I speak to (at my book signing events), publishing professionals and fantasy authors to describe the 'epic fantasy' of the 1990s, as seen on such websites as www.vision.ae and The Caffeinated Symposium.

5. As detailed in the introduction to this exegesis.

a fight against a repressive Establishment[6], the creative expression of individuality, diversity and difference, the introduction of a new and distinct authorial voice, and the successful contribution of a new sub-genre to the wider genre of fantasy.

---

6. Including its dominant business models, as described in the introduction to this exegesis.

6. Conclusion

To conclude, this exegesis has shown how the sub-genres of fantasy are informed by, and a reaction to, their sociohistorical moment. They are also informed by, and a reaction to, the sub-genres that precede them. In terms of 'metaphysical fantasy', it emerged specifically in the mid to late 2000s, at a time when the UK was experiencing economic, political, social and moral turmoil. In such a context, the 'Chosen One', class structure, judgemental morality and social stability of the 'epic fantasy' kingdom were exposed as redundant and/or false. What 'metaphysical fantasy' offered instead was a psychologically fraught protagonist (anti-hero), social change, a moral ambivalence and the tolerance of difference. In doing so, 'metaphysical fantasy' laid the foundations for the subsequent second-world fantasy sub-genre of 'grimdark fantasy', a sub-genre which presents a survivalist as protagonist, an expedient sense of morality, uncompromising behaviours and extreme outrage.

At the same time, it is shown how far second-world fantasy has come since the days of the original British 'high fantasy' of Tolkien's *The Lord of the Rings*. Where 'high fantasy' tends to offer an omniscient narrator, a singular and epic worldview, Christian values, a Satanic antagonist, a Christ-like 'Chosen One' and a lack of irony, 'metaphysical fantasy' presents us with a plurality of narrative point of view, a subversion of religious doctrine, ambiguous and inconstant characters, and plenty of irony and dark humour. Indeed, the 'problem' of religion and the theme of competing philosophies of being is more distinct in 'metaphysical fantasy' than in any other sub-genre to date. In this sense, 'metaphysical fantasy' could be described as the first 'post-Christian' sub-genre of fantasy, its ultimate concern not the prescription of particular social behaviours but a philosophical consideration of the individual's place in the cosmos. 'Metaphysical fantasy' does not presume to provide answers to its consideration, describing a more modern (Millennial) experience than 'epic fantasy'. Unlike later 'grimdark fantasy', however, 'metaphysical fantasy' tends to culminate optimistically with an understanding of the importance of friendship, fidelity and knowledge of others, tolerating challenge and difference, and celebrating subversive humour and the courage to act.

Where the self-published but best-selling *Necromancer's Gambit* began the development of 'metaphysical fantasy', I would say *Empire of the Saviours* – which secured a global three-book deal with the UK's market leader in fantasy publishing, was translated into German by Random House and was long-listed for the UK's national fantasy award – truly focussed and best articulated the themes, relevance, motifs, characterisation, plot and literary style of 'metaphysical fantasy'. *Empire of the Saviours* was the book that finally established the distinct and valuable contribution of 'metaphysical fantasy' to the wider fantasy genre. Indeed, it was following the publication of *Empire of the Saviours* that other authors began to publish work using or described by the label of 'metaphysical fantasy', including Neil Gaiman[1], Taya Wood[2], Jim Murdoch[3], Robin Coe[4], James Riley[5],

---

1. *American Gods: The Tenth Anniversary Edition: A Novel* on www.amazon.co.uk is categorised under and tagged with 'Metaphysical & Visionary' fantasy.
2. Wood, T. (2009). 'Taya Wood', *Twitter*. Available at: www.twitter.com/tayawood, (Accessed: 12 July 2016).
3. Murdoch, J. (2015). *What is Metaphysical Fantasy?* Available at: www.jmurdoch.com/what-is-metaphysical-fantasy, (Accessed: 12 July 2016).
4. Coe, R. (2010). 'Robin Coe', *Twitter*. Available at: www.twitter.com/robin_coe, (Accessed: 12 July 2016).
5. Swinyard, H. (2016). '#MetaphysicalFantasy', Twitter, 9 January. Available at: www.twitter.com/search?q=%Metaphysicalfantasy&src=typd, (Accessed: 12 July 2016).

David Lindsay[6], and the list goes on.

> *Beware those who speak of faith and the betterment of the people yet say magic is the work of the devil.* (*Empire of the Saviours,* p. v)

6. Valentine, M. (2015). *The Universal Witch.* Available at: www.wormwoodiana.blogspot.co.uk/2015_10_01_archive.html, (Accessed: 12 July 2016).

7. References

Abercrombie, J. (2006). *The Blade Itself: The First Law*. London: Gollancz.

AIDS.gov. (2011). *A Timeline of HIV/AIDS*. Available at: https://www.aids.gov/hiv-aids-basics/hiv-aids-101/aids-timeline/, (Accessed: 11 July 2016).

Aldiss, B. (1970). *The Moment of Eclipse*. London: Faber and Faber.

Bakker, R. S. (2004). *The Darkness That Comes Before*. London: Orbit.

Brett, P. V. (2008). *The Painted Man: The Demon Cycle*. London: Voyager Books.

Buffy the Vampire Slayer. (1997). The WB Television Network, 10 March.

Campbell, A. (2006). *Scar Night*. New York: Tor.

Canavan, T. (2004). *The Magicians' Guild*. London: Orbit.

Canavan, T. (2005). *The High Lord*. London: Orbit.

Canavan, T. (2005). *The Novice*. London: Orbit.

Carpenter, H. (1977). *J. R. R. Tolkien: A Biography*. New York: Ballantine Books.

Carpenter, H. and Tolkien, C. (eds.) (1981). *The Letters of J. R. R. Tolkien*. London: George Allen & Unwin.

Coe, R. (2010). 'Robin Coe', *Twitter*. Available at: www. twitter.com/robin_coe, (Accessed: 12 July 2016).

Collins, S. (2008). *The Hunger Games*. New York: Scholastic Press.

Conan the Barbarian. (1982). [Movie release]. Universal Pictures, 14 May.

Cooper, S. (1965). *Over Sea, Under Stone*. London: Jonathan Cape.

Dalton, A. J. (2008). *Metaphysical Fantasy*. Available at: www.ajdalton.eu, (Accessed: 15 July 2016).

Dalton, A. J. (2008). *Necromancer's Gambit: Book One of The Flesh & Bone Trilogy*. Milton Keynes: AuthorHouse UK.

Dalton, A. J. (2009). *Necromancer's Betrayal: Book Two of The Flesh & Bone Trilogy*. Milton Keynes: AuthorHouse UK.

Dalton, A. J. (2010). *Necromancer's fall: Book Three of The*

Flesh & Bone Trilogy. Milton Keynes: AuthorHouse UK.

Dalton, A. J. (2012). *Empire of the Saviours: Book One: Chronicles of a Cosmic Warlord*. London: Gollancz.

Dalton, A. J. (2013). *Gateway of the Saviours: Book Two: Chronicles of a Cosmic Warlord*. London: Gollancz.

Dalton, A. J. (2014). *Tithe of the Saviours: Book Three: Chronicles of a Cosmic Warlord*. London: Gollancz.

Dashner, J. (2009). *The Maze Runner*. New York: Delacorte Press.

Di Filippo, P. (1995). *The Steampunk Trilogy*. New York: Four Walls Eight Windows.

Donaldson, S. (1977). *Lord Foul's Bane: An Epic Fantasy*. New York: Holt, Rinehart and Winston.

Eddings, D. (1982). *Pawn of Prophecy*. New York: Del Rey Books.

Feist, R. (1982). *Magician*. New York: Doubleday.

Freud, S. and Breuer, J. (1895). *Studies on Hysteria*. Leipzig and Vienna: Franz Deuticke.

Freud, S. (1899). *The Interpretation of Dreams*. Leipzig and Vienna: Franz Deuticke.

Furey, M. (1994). Aurian: *The Artefacts of Power*. New York: Bantam Books.

Gaiman, N. (1996). *Neverwhere*. London: BBC Books.

Gaiman, N. (2011). *American Gods: The Tenth Anniversary Edition: A Novel*. New York: HarperCollins Publishers.

Garner, A. (1967). *The Owl Service*. London: William Collins, Sons.

Gemmell, D. (1984). *Legend*. New York: Century.

Goodkind, T. (1994). *Wizard's First Rule*. New York: Tor Fantasy.

Hampson, F. (1950). 'Dan Dare', *The Eagle*. London: Hulton Press.

Hobb, R. (1995). *Assassin's Apprentice*. London: Voyager Books.

Howard, R. E. (1932). 'The Phoenix on the Sword', *Weird Tales*. Chicago: J. C. Henneberger.

Howe, N. and Strauss, W. (1991). *Generations: The History of America's Future, 1584 to 2069*. New York: William Morrow.

Howe, N. and Strauss, W. (2000). *Millennials Rising: The Next Generation*. New York: Vintage.

Hunt, S. (1994). *For the Crown and the Dragon*. London: Green Nebula Publishing.

Jackson, S. and Livingstone, I. (1982). *The Warlock of Firetop Mountain: Fighting Fantasy Series*. London: Puffin Books.

Jeter, K. (1979). *Morlock Night*. London: Duncan Baird Publishers.

Jeter, K. (1987). *Science Fiction Citations*. Available at: http://www.jessesword.com/sf/view/327, (Accessed: 11 July 2016).

Jones, J. V. (1995). *The Baker's Boy*. New York: Aspect.

Komarck, M. (2015). *In Defence of the Chosen One*. Available at: http://fantasy-faction.com/2015/in-defence-of-the-chosen-one, (Accessed: 11 July 2016).

Lackey, M. (1991). *Winds of Fate*. New York: DAW.

Lawrence, M. (2011). *Prince of Thorns: The Broken Empire Trilogy*. London: HarperCollins UK.

Le Guin, U. (1968). *A Wizard of Earthsea*. Berkeley: Parnassus Press.

Lewis, C. S. (1950). *The Lion, the Witch and the Wardrobe*. London: Bles.

Martin, G. R. R. (1996). *A Game of Thrones: A Song of Ice and Fire*. London: Voyager Books.

McKenna, J. E. (1999). *The Thief's Gamble*. London: Orbit.

Meyer, S. (2005). *Twilight*. New York: Little, Brown and Co.

Meyer, S. (2006). *New Moon*. New York: Little, Brown and Co.

Meyer, S. (2007). *Eclipse*. New York: Little, Brown and Co.

Meyer, S. (2008). *Breaking Dawn*. New York: Little, Brown and Co.

Modesitt Jr., L. E. (1991). *The Magic of Recluce*. Charlotte, NC: Paw Prints.

Moorcock, M. (1970). *The Eternal Champion*. New York: Dell Books.

Moorcock, M. (1974). *The Hollow Lands*. New York: Harper and Row.

Murdoch, J. (2015). *What is Metaphysical Fantasy?*

Available at: www.jmurdoch.com/what-is-metaphysical-fantasy, (Accessed: 12 July 2016).

Neverwhere. (1996). BBC Radio 2, 12 September.

Niven, L. (1970). *Ringworld*. New York: Ballantine Books.

Norman, J. (1966). *The Tarnsman of Gor*. New York: Ballantine Books.

Perry, A. (2013). *Hodderscape Review Project*. Available at: http://www.hodderscape.co.uk/hodderscape-review-project/, (Accessed: 14 July 2016).

Polidori, J. (1819). *The Vampyre*. London: Sherwood, Neely and Jones.

Pratchett, T. (2011). *Snuff*. New York: Doubleday.

Shelley, M. (1818). *Frankenstein: The Modern Prometheus*. London: Lackington, Hughes, Harding, Mavor, & Jones.

Smith, A. G. (2010). *Lockdown: Escape from Furnace*. New York: Tor.

Soars, J. and Soars, L. (1987). *Headway: Upper-intermediate*. Oxford: Oxford University Press.

Stableford, B. (2005). *The A to Z of Fantasy Literature*. Plymouth: Scarecrow Press.

Stevenson, R. L. (1886). *Strange Case of Dr Jekyll and Mr Hyde*. London: Longmans, Green and Co.

Stoker, B. (1897). *Dracula*. London: Archibald Constable and Co.

Swinyard, H. (2016). '#MetaphysicalFantasy', *Twitter*, 9 January. Available at: www.twitter.com/ search?q=%Metaphysicalfantasy&src=typd, (Accessed: 12 July 2016).

The Book Plank. (2014). *Author Interview with Stephen Hunt*. Available at: http://thebookplank.blogspot. co.uk/2014/05/author-interview-with-stephen-hunt.html, (Accessed: 15 July 2016).

The Caffeinated Symposium. (2011). *Fantasy: 1990-2000: The Age of the Doorstops and Gimmicks*. Available at: http://caffeinesymposium.blogspot.co.uk/2011/07/fantasy-1990-2000-age-of-doorstops-and.html, (Accessed: 15 July 2016).

Tolkien, J. R. R. (1937). *The Hobbit, or There and Back*. London: George Allen & Unwin.

Tolkien, J. R. R. (1954). *The Fellowship of the Ring: Being the First Part of The Lord of the Rings*. London: George Allen & Unwin.

Tolkien, J. R. R. (1954). *The Two Towers: Being the Second Part of The Lord of the Rings*. London: George Allen & Unwin.

Tolkien, J. R. R. (1955). *The Return of the King: Being the Third Part of The Lord of the Rings*. London: George Allen & Unwin.

Tolkien, J. R. R. and Tolkien, C. (1977). *The Silmarillion*. London: Allen and Unwin.

True blood. (2008). HBO, 7 September.

Twilight. (2008). [Movie release]. Summit Entertainment, 21 November.

Valentine, M. (2015). *The Universal Witch*. Available at: www.wormwoodiana.blogspot.co.uk/2015_10_01_archive. html, (Accessed: 12 July 2016).

Vance, J. (1973). *Trullion: Alastor 2262*. New York: Ballantine Books.

Vernes, J. (1873). *Twenty Thousand Leagues under the Seas*. London: Sampson Low, Marston, Low and Searle.

Vision. (2015). *Joe Abercrombie's Fantasy Land*. Available at: http://vision.ae/articles/joe_abercrombies_fantasy_land, (Accessed: 15 July 2016).

Walpole, Horace (1764). *The Castle of Otranto: A Gothic Story*. London: William Bathoe.

Wells, H. G. (1895). *The Time Machine*. London: William Heinemann.

Wells, H. G. (1898). *The War of the Worlds*. London: William Heinemann.

Whitaker, D. (1973). *Doctor Who and the Daleks*. London: Target Books.

Wood, T. (2009). 'Taya Wood', *Twitter*. Available at: www.twitter.com/tayawood, (Accessed: 12 July 2016).

Wyndham, J. (1951). *The Day of the Triffids*. London: Michael Joseph.

Wyndham, J. (1957). *The Midwich Cuckoos*. London: Michael Joseph.

Young, J. (2005). Terry Pratchett on the Origins of Discworld, His Order of the British Empire and Everything in between, *Science Fiction Weekly*, 449.

Zimmer Bradley, M., May, J. and Norton, A. (1990). *Black Trillium*. New York: Bantam Books.

Lightning Source UK Ltd.
Milton Keynes UK
UKOW05f0903260117
292922UK00006B/72/P